The *Adventures*
Larry the Lunchbox Lizard

First Time With a Babysitter

Written by **Matt Chandler**
Illustrated by **Leah Lewis**

To my mom, Christine Chandler

For always believing in me

Printed in the United States of America
Zoliver Press, New York
ISBN-13: 978-0692401408
The Adventures of Larry the Lunchbox Lizard – First Time With a Babysitter
Chandler, Matt –First Printing, March 2015

www.lunchboxlarry.com
www.mattchandlerwriting.com

Introduction

For Will, being four-years-old is hard. Whether it is moving with his family to a new town, having his first babysitter, learning to swim, or going to the doctor, Will has lots of stuff going on. Lucky for him, he has his friend Larry.

Larry isn't like the other kids in the neighborhood. He is tiny, green, and he has a tail. Larry is a lizard, but more than that, he's Will's best friend. He lives in Will's lunchbox, always nearby in case his buddy needs help.

Together, Will and Larry learn that you can do anything you want and nothing is too scary when you have a friend by your side.

Will was supposed to be taking his nap. But he couldn't sleep.

He was listening to his mom and dad in the next room, and he didn't like what he heard.

"I'll call Diane and see if her daughter Kelly can babysit," he heard his mom say. "She loves Will, and besides, it will only be for a few hours."

Will had never had a babysitter before. Well, his grandma came over if his parents went out, but she wasn't a babysitter.

She always brought him chocolate chip cookies and let him watch cartoons all night.

Will loved to lie down on the couch and fall asleep while his grandma told him stories. She was the best storyteller ever. But a babysitter, no way!

Will slid out from under the covers and tiptoed over to the bookshelf in the corner of his room. He reached up and carefully pulled down his lunchbox.

The more he thought about it, the more his tummy felt like there were a hundred worms wrestling inside. He was scared.

He made sure he held it flat and didn't tip it. He flipped up the metal hinge that held the cover in place and gently lifted the lid.

Larry was sleeping as usual. Will always woke his friend up the same way: he took his pointer finger and rubbed Larry's belly. Soon he began to wiggle and his eyes opened.

"Hi Will, what's going on?" Larry said.

Will told Larry what he had heard.

"Can you believe they are going to make me have a babysitter?" he said.

"But you like Kelly," Larry said. "She is nice."

She might be nice, but she wasn't his grandma, and Will didn't want her to babysit him.

"Think about it Will," Larry said, as he climbed out of the lunchbox and sat next to Will on the bed.

"Kelly might not bake you cookies, but I bet she will play games with you.

And, you won't have to take a bath like you do when grandma watches you."

Will thought about what his friend said. He really didn't like bath time. And even though grandma made him cookies, she didn't like to play his favorite games. Still, he wished his mom and dad could just stay home with him.

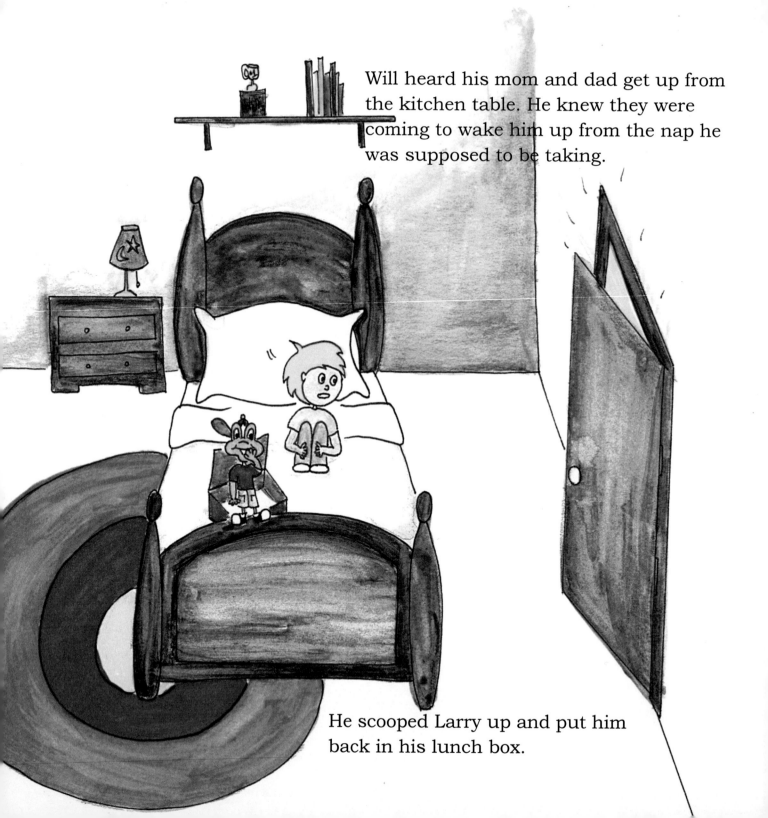

Will heard his mom and dad get up from the kitchen table. He knew they were coming to wake him up from the nap he was supposed to be taking.

He scooped Larry up and put him back in his lunch box.

As Will carried his friend back to his shelf, Larry called out from inside his lunchbox.

"Don't worry buddy, I'll be with you. It will be fun, you'll see."

Will's mom gently shook his shoulder, and he pretended to wake up.

"Sweetie, your dad and I have to go out tonight and grandma can't come over, so you are going to have your first babysitter.

Isn't that exciting?"

Will thought about what Larry said and even though his stomach still felt like it was full of worms, he didn't say anything.

"Kelly from across the street is going to watch you," Will's mom said. "I bet you two will have lots of fun!"

Just then there was a knock at the door. Will heard his dad talking and he heard Kelly's voice.

"Will, come down, Kelly's here," his dad yelled up the stairs.

Will grabbed his lunchbox before he headed downstairs.
Larry tapped on the inside, and Will stopped and popped it open.

"It's going to be great Will," Larry said.
"Just remember, I'm right here with you."

Before he knew it, Will's mom and dad had hugged and kissed him and were out the door.

His tummy hurt even more.

"So sweetie, what do you want to do for fun?" Kelly said.

Will didn't say anything.

"I bet you like to play hide and seek," Kelly said.

Will couldn't believe it. He LOVED hide and seek! "Um, okay," he said, shyly.

"Great, you hide and I will try and find you," Kelly said.

She covered her eyes and began to count. Will grabbed Larry and ran into his bedroom. He crawled under the bed and froze in place.

"Ready or not, here I come," Kelly called.

Will watched as Kelly came into his room. He could see her feet as she searched for him. Larry poked his head out.

"See, I told you this would be great," he whispered.

Just then, Kelly bent down and came face to face with Will.

"Gotcha!" she shouted. Will giggled.
Maybe Larry was right, having a
babysitter *could* be fun.

Playing hide and seek made Will hungry. He asked Kelly if she could make him a snack.

"Oh, I almost forgot, I brought you a surprise," Kelly said. "My mom baked some cookies today, and I brought the extras with me!"

"What kind are they?" Will asked.

"Chocolate chip," Kelly said.

Will smiled, "My favorite!"

Kelly piled the cookies on a plate and poured two glasses of milk.

"Let's pick out a cartoon to watch," she said.

Will took a big bite of his cookie and then snuggled up with Kelly to watch his favorite cartoon.

While she was busy flipping channels, Will snuck a cookie and opened his lunchbox.

"You were right," he said to Larry, dropping a cookie inside his lunchbox. "Having a babysitter can be lots of fun."

Larry tried to say something, but he couldn't. His cheeks were stuffed!

When the show was over, Will asked Kelly
if she would tell him a story.

"Sure Will," she said.

Kelly picked a story about a strong prince
who had to fight an army of giants to save a princess
who was trapped in a scary castle.

Will liked the story, especially the ending. The prince and princess rode away on his big white horse.

Will loved horses. His dad said maybe someday they could get a horse now that they lived in the country.

Just as Kelly finished her story, Will heard a car pull in. Then, the front door opened and his mom and dad walked in.

"Hi Will, how did your first time go?" his dad asked.

"It was great," Will said. "Can Kelly watch me again?"

"Sure," his mom said. "It sure sounds like you two had a fun night!"

"OK champ, time for
bed," Will's dad said as
he scooped Will up off
the couch.

"Don't forget my
lunchbox," Will said.

His dad handed him his lunchbox and up the stairs they went.

After his dad tucked him in to bed, Will reached over and opened his lunchbox. Larry stuck his head out. There were lots of cookie crumbs inside the lunchbox.

"You were right Larry," Will said. "Having a babysitter was great. Thanks for helping me."

"That's what friends are for," Larry said. "Next time Kelly comes to babysit you, can I have *two* cookies?"

"Deal," Will said.

He closed his eyes and drifted off to sleep wondering how soon Kelly could come back and babysit him again.

Made in the USA
Middletown, DE
17 March 2015